THE HOUSEMAID'S WEDDING

A SHORT STORY

FREIDA McFADDEN

Cover design by Freida McFadden
Cover images © lyashko/Adobe Stock, creativefamily/Adobe Stock, Kateryna Mostova/Shutterstock, Ilina93/Shutterstock

Published by Poisoned Pen Press, an imprint of Sourcebooks
1935 Brookdale RD, Naperville, IL 60563–2773
(630) 961-3900
sourcebooks.com

Originally self-published in 2024 by Freida McFadden.

Cataloging-in-Publication Data is on file with the Library of Congress.

Printed and bound in the United States of America.
LSC 10 9 8 7 6 5 4 3 2 1

ALSO BY FREIDA MCFADDEN

Dear Debbie
The Intruder
The Tenant
The Crash
The Boyfriend
The Teacher
The Coworker
Ward D
Never Lie
The Inmate
The Housemaid
The Housemaid's Secret
The Housemaid Is Watching
Do You Remember?
Do Not Disturb
The Locked Door
Want to Know a Secret?
One by One
The Wife Upstairs
The Perfect Son
The Ex
The Surrogate Mother
Brain Damage
Dead Med

This one is for all my readers.
Somehow, you got me to write four of these.

AUTHOR'S NOTE

I wrote *The Housemaid's Wedding* as a short story to fill in the long gap between book 2 (*The Housemaid's Secret*) and book 3 (*The Housemaid Is Watching*) of the Housemaid series. I was worried readers might feel cheated that they never got to see Millie and Enzo tie the knot, so here it is! This can be read either between books 2 and 3, or after book 3.

Also, please keep in mind that this is not a full-length book. I wrote this to be bonus material so you can learn a little more about what happened to Millie and Enzo between books 2 and 3.

With that in mind, I hope you enjoy this little glimpse back into Millie's life!

PROLOGUE

This man is going to kill me.

There is murder in his eyes. I've seen enough in my lifetime to recognize the danger that I'm in. This man will not wait for an explanation. He will not even allow me a split second to catch my breath. He will *end* me.

It's just the two of us in this stifling, claustrophobic space. He made certain of that—he stalked me and waited until the moment I was alone, then he locked the door behind us. Now here we are.

And he can do whatever he wants to me. Nobody knows I'm here.

My nose is bruised, possibly broken. Blood streams from my nostrils in warm rivulets, dripping down my lips. It tastes metallic. Slamming his fist into my nose is one of the first things he did to me, before even saying hello. It was his way of letting me know he means business.

“I will break every single bone in your body,” he hisses at me.

He means it. Oh God, he *definitely* means it.

I never thought my day would end up this way. If I had known—if I had any idea at all what this man would do to me—I would have made very different decisions this morning. I thought I could handle this, but from the beginning, I was in over my head. I had no idea.

It’s my fault I’m here. I made a terrible mistake.

And now it’s too late.

ONE

MILLIE

I'm going to cut your throat, Millie Calloway."

Those words are *not* how you want to be woken up in the morning.

But here I am, groggy from the deep, dream-filled sleep that I was wrenched from by this early-morning phone call. I'm holding the phone to my ear, wondering if the harsh whispered threat I just heard was part of a dream I was still having. After all, who gets woken up by somebody promising to cut their throat?

Well, me, apparently.

"Excuse me?" I say into the phone, my voice still scratchy with sleep.

I roll over in bed to prop up on my side, rubbing my eyes to wake myself up. Maybe I heard them wrong. Maybe instead of cutting my throat, the stranger on the other end of the line actually wants to cut the costs of my car insurance.

"You heard me," the male voice growls, low and

ominous. "You stuck your nose in the *wrong* place, and now you're going to pay the price." A brief pause follows for me to absorb this new piece of information, and then:

"I'm going to kill you slowly and painfully, Millie Calloway."

Nope, not a dream. This is most definitely real and clearly meant for me, as evidenced by the repeated use of my full name. I can't pretend this is some sort of wrong number or spam call. But it's not the first death threat I have received, and it won't be the last.

I'm not thrilled about the fact that it arrived on my wedding day though.

They say rain on your wedding day is good luck. Death threats on your wedding day? Probably not so much. Still, I know exactly how to deal with this asshole.

"Go to hell," I reply calmly, then I jam my thumb into the red button on the screen to end the call.

I toss my phone back onto the nightstand, where it has spent the evening charging, next to the mouth guard that is supposed to keep me from grinding my teeth at night, if I could ever remember to pop it in before bedtime. I refuse to let that call get to me. I have a tendency to do things that piss people off, and occasional death threats are to be expected, but they have never proven to be more than empty words. It's something I've grown used to.

I will *not* let it ruin this day.

I roll my head to look over at my fiancé, who is stirring beside me. Enzo might have been awakened by the ringing of my phone, but thank God, he did not hear what that jerk said to me. If he had any inkling that somebody was threatening me, he'd be furious. He would have made a big deal out of it—maybe even suggested going to the *police*—and that's the last thing I want today. Like I said, it was surely just empty words.

Today will not be about some insecure asshole. Today is going to be about me and Enzo becoming husband and wife.

"Millie?" he murmurs, his Italian-accented voice thick with sleep. "Who was on the phone?"

"Telemarketer," I lie.

He grimaces because he hates calls from telemarketers. He would've hated the actual call even more, but he's never going to find out about it. If it happens again, I'll have to tell him eventually, but not today.

Enzo rubs his eyes as he struggles into a sitting position. His black hair is sticking up, and he's got a day's worth of stubble on his jaw, but my fiancé is at his sexiest first thing in the morning. And that's saying *a lot* because his baseline level of sexiness is quite high. Then the covers fall away to reveal the taut muscles in his chest, and I forget all about that stupid call.

In only four short hours, this man is going to be my husband. My *husband*. We're going to be married, with rings and everything. Despite the fact that we've been a couple for a long time and been through hell together, I never entirely believed this day would ever come.

I place a hand gently on the swell of my abdomen. Try as I might, I can't forget that *this* is why we're getting married. When he popped the question, Enzo made a whole speech about how he knew from the second he met me that I was the one and how he wanted to spend his whole life devoted to me, but he proposed *one week* after I told him I was pregnant. The timing was unmistakable.

"How are you feeling?" He noticed me touching my belly, and his brow creases in concern. "Still with the nausea?"

Enzo was a rock star during my horrific bout of first-trimester nausea. He bought me three forms of ginger, which sadly only confirmed three times that I hate ginger. He bought a diffuser because he read aromatherapy can work, but it did not. He even read a book about acupressure and gave me a personal session, which resulted in a sexy outcome that admittedly *did* help me forget about my nausea for a little while. But nothing worked. Until about a month ago, I was throwing up every day. Sometimes multiple times a day. It wasn't fun.

But it's like they say—what doesn't kill you makes you stronger. If I can deal with twice-daily vomiting, I can deal with some chickenshit asshole threatening me on the phone.

Besides, I know who that guy is. Okay, I might not know his name, but over the last several years, I have helped quite a few women escape their abusive husbands. In the process, I have gained some enemies in the form of angry husbands. I don't know which of those husbands was threatening to slit my throat, but it was almost certainly one of them.

"I'm fine." I manage a smile that initially feels forced, but when I see the smile on his own lips, it becomes genuine. "I'm just excited about today."

"Me too." He reaches for me, pulling me into his bare arms and drawing me close. "I can't wait to marry you."

When he says those words, I feel—dare I say

it?—*lucky*. I've never felt lucky in my whole life—it's not a word I'd ever have used to describe myself. But at this moment, I feel like the luckiest woman in the world.

Okay, nothing about this wedding is conventional. It's not going to be a big ceremony—we will get married at Manhattan's City Hall in a tiny chapel that I've read is more like a conference room with a few decorations. Also, there's that whole part about me being knocked up. But who cares? What matters is that the two of us are going to spend the rest of our lives together, and there's no one else I would rather share that journey with.

Also, there's one more thing that will make this day special.

TWO

Millie?" Enzo speaks the word into my hair as he cuddles close to me in bed. "Is sex on the morning of the wedding bad luck?"

Good question. As badly as I want the answer to be no, I am desperate for my run of good luck to continue.

"Probably," I admit.

His face falls. "You are sure?"

"You know," I say, "we're not even supposed to *see* each other today."

"Really?" Enzo looks around our tiny living space, clearly confused. We occupy a small one-bedroom apartment in the Bronx, where the living room and kitchen are merged into one. "Where am I supposed to go to not see you?"

"It's more of a rule for fancy people who have friends with guest bedrooms where they can spend the night."

"I hate fancy people." He kisses my neck, which

makes my whole body tingle. "So since we *already* broke rules, it is not bad to break more, yes?"

Bad luck or not, on any other day, I would be powerless to resist him. But today is my wedding day. I have to shower and make sure my dress fits well and get my hair looking respectable and put on more makeup than my usual dash of drugstore lipstick. It takes all my self-restraint to push him away. "Better not. I need to get ready."

"Get ready?" He looks baffled. "But our wedding is not for four hours!"

"Right. It's in *only four hours*."

Enzo is frowning, but he reluctantly relinquishes his grasp on me so that I can go to the bathroom and take a shower. Men just don't get it. I had to iron the white shirt he'll be wearing today because such a thing didn't even occur to him, despite the fact that it was *clearly* unacceptably wrinkled. He will shower in five minutes, towel off his hair, throw on his suit, and the whole process will be done in less than ten minutes.

But I need to look perfect today. Because there's one other thing that will make this day incredibly special.

My *parents* are coming to the wedding.

This is a *really* big deal. My parents and I are not close. In fact, I haven't seen them in well over a decade. They abandoned me in my time of need back when I was a teenager, when I defended my best friend from being attacked and ended up in prison for killing the bastard that did it. They threw me to the wolves—didn't give me a penny for my defense and never came to visit me when I was locked away. And even after all that, I was willing to forgive and forget—they are my parents, after all—but they were not. *You're a bad apple, Millie. We don't want you poisoning our lives anymore.*

Do you know what it feels like for your parents to call you a poisoned apple? It doesn't feel great. Yet, no matter how much they pushed me away, I still craved their support. I loved them, and more than anything, I wanted them to see I had changed from the girl I used to be.

I had been worried I'd never see them again. And I was sad that since Enzo's entire family is either deceased or back in Sicily, he would have no family members at our wedding. I told this to Enzo one night, not long after his proposal. He was the one who convinced me to call my parents to let them know about the wedding and the baby.

My mother did not sound excited when she realized I was on the other end of the line. At first, I thought she might hang up on me. But when I told her I was trying to get my degree in social work, she thawed considerably. She wasn't thrilled to hear I was pregnant out of wedlock, but she was glad to know that I'd soon be marrying the father of the baby. And when I extended a wedding invitation, she told me she would be there. My parents will be our only guests—the only witnesses to our holy matrimony.

I'm so nervous about seeing them after all this time. I'm scared I'll say the wrong words and screw things up all over again. But I'm also excited. I love my parents, and I always hoped that they would forgive me for my sins of the past, especially since I honestly don't think they were such grievous sins.

And no, this isn't exactly how I dreamed my wedding

would be when I was a little girl, but I still want it to be as perfect as it can possibly be. We've already started the day with a death threat, so we have a lot of ground to make up.

I roll out of bed, tugging on my oversized T-shirt, which is feeling decidedly less oversized lately. Before hitting the bathroom, I walk over to the window to discover snowflakes have started to fall from the sky. It's only the beginning of December, and the weather forecast didn't predict snow, but it's coming down fast enough to stick to the ground.

Is snow on your wedding day good luck? Or is it only rain? Or is rain just *ironic*?

Enzo yawns, still in the bed. "Hey," he says, "how about Felicity?"

"Felicity?" I repeat.

"What is wrong with Felicity?"

I shrug. "I don't know. It's just not my favorite name in the whole world."

"Okay, then you tell me, what *is* your favorite name in the whole world?"

Ever since we found out at our last OB/GYN appointment that we're having a baby girl, we have at least three conversations every day about baby names. Or more accurately, we have at least three conversations every day where one of us suggests a baby name and the other explains why it sucks. Presumably, we will manage to agree on something in the next four months, or else our baby girl will go through life nameless.

"Let's put a pin in the baby name discussion for now," I say. "I need to take a shower."

"But I like Felicity."

"Yeah, well, *I* liked Nadine."

Enzo makes a face. "Okay. We put the pin in it for now."

I'm about to head into the bathroom to shower when my phone starts ringing again. Enzo glances at it and starts to pick it up for me, but I make a mad dash across the room to snatch it up before he can.

When I get a look at the screen, I'm glad I didn't let Enzo answer the call. The 718 number flashing is unfamiliar, and I'm almost positive it's the same number that woke me up this morning. I send the call to voicemail. I'm not in the mood for another death threat.

"Spam again," I say.

He nods sympathetically but doesn't ask any questions. And he has a right to ask questions, especially when I take the phone with me into the bathroom. It's a weird thing to do, but I can't risk him picking up and hearing that man telling me he's going to cut my throat. Enzo will lose his *mind* if he hears that—he will not just shrug it off and go about his day.

I'll tell him all about it—tomorrow.

I take a quick shower, noticing that my belly has popped out a lot more in the last week. A month ago, you couldn't tell I was pregnant at all, even without any clothes on. At worst, it looked like I had a food baby. But it's becoming increasingly obvious that something is growing inside me.

My baby.

Little Nadine.

Or not. But definitely not Felicity.

After I finish my shower, I leave the bathroom, wrapped in a skimpy towel. Enzo is still in bed, scrolling on his phone as I make my way to the closet, where my wedding dress is hung up inside.

As we are not having a traditional wedding, I do not have a traditional wedding dress. First of all, it's not white. I *hate* that color, and not only that, it seems wildly inappropriate given my...situation. So a few weeks ago, I went to Macy's and purchased an A-line silhouette pale-blue dress with lace sleeves. It was marked down from nearly three hundred dollars to just over one hundred, which was barely in our budget, but I bought it anyway, because, for God's sake, it's our wedding. Plus, the dress can serve as both my "something new" and my "something blue."

It also has a scoop neck, which will be perfect to show off my "something old," which will be a gold locket necklace that my mother is bringing me. The necklace is an heirloom passed down from her mother, and her mother before her. Honestly, I never thought she would ever pass that necklace on to me. And it means much more that I'll be receiving it on my wedding day.

"You're not supposed to see me in this dress." I cast a worried look at Enzo. "It's bad luck."

"I'm not supposed to see you at all," he reminds me. "Anyway, I saw it already. Remember? You did fashion show when you came home."

"Oh, right." That makes me feel a little better. "I guess I should stop being so superstitious."

He grins at me. "It is cute. Anyway, this is your wedding day. You are allowed to be *pazza*."

He has used that word multiple times to refer to me. I haven't looked it up because I'm not sure I want to know. I don't think it's a compliment, but I let it slide.

The towel falls from my body, and Enzo lets out an appreciative whistle. I take the blue dress off the hanger and slide my legs into the silky fabric. I purchased a brand-new pair of pantyhose just for today, and then an extra pair in case I get a rip. I have thought of everything. I am prepared for any emergency. Today is going to be perfect.

Except…

Oh no. This stupid dress doesn't zip up anymore!

THREE

What is wrong?"

Enzo looks at me with concern as I struggle with the zipper. I tried the dress on only one week ago, and it was fine. It fit *perfectly*. So why am I struggling now?

"Can you zip me up?" I ask him.

He jumps off the bed, eager to help. He's wearing only a pair of boxers, and it distracts me for a moment from my distress about the zipper, but then he is behind me, and the distraction is gone. His fingers linger on the small of my back.

"Last chance for sexy time," he breathes in my ear.

I'm a little tempted, but I shake my head. "Just zip up the dress."

That's when things get real. Enzo tries his best, bless his heart. He struggles to pull up the zipper without ripping the fabric, but nothing is happening. It's not budging. Over the last week, my stomach has grown to the point where this dress no longer fits.

"I am sorry." He lowers his hands in defeat. "It does not go."

I bury my face in my palms and sink down onto our bed. "Oh my God, what am I going to do?"

He frowns. "Another dress?"

I shake my head. "I don't have anything else that looks good."

"You look beautiful in everything."

His voice is so earnest that I want to cry. He's trying his best to make light of a bad situation, but there's no fixing it. There's nothing else in my closet that is wedding appropriate. I had *one* decent dress to wear today, and now it doesn't fit me anymore. I can't afford a second dress. I couldn't even afford the first dress.

I suppose I could go back to Macy's and try to exchange it. Except I bought the dress weeks ago, and it seemed to leave more than enough room for growth, so I tossed the receipt. I had no idea I'd suddenly "pop" over the last week. Anyway, I can't try to return it now—the last thing I want is to go into some store and be accused of stealing the dress. What if they call the police? What if I go to *jail* on my wedding day? That's even worse than a death threat. Or at least, it's *as* bad.

"I really wanted this dress," is all I say.

"Okay, then." Enzo sits beside me on the bed and takes my hand in his. "Give me the dress, and I will fix it."

"Oh, I didn't realize you were a seamstress."

His lips twitch. "I know a guy who is a tailor. He owes me favor."

I am highly skeptical, but what can I do? Either Enzo's friend will come through, or I will get married in jeans and a T-shirt. Okay, I have a nice skirt and blouse I could wear. But it's not my pretty blue dress.

Enzo calls his friend right away, who amazingly thinks he can get it done in time for the ceremony, which is now in *only three hours*. He asks for a bunch of measurements, which Enzo takes using the tape measure from his tool kit. Then he leaves with the numbers scribbled on a scrap of paper, my dress in a plastic bag, and his car keys, promising to be back in half an hour.

Honestly, I don't understand why I couldn't go with him to have the measurements taken by a professional, but Enzo had some convoluted reason why I couldn't visit his friend. When he tried to explain it to me in Italian, I gave up. It seems impossible that this dress will be ready in time, but I have to admit, Enzo rarely fails me.

While he's gone, I return to the bathroom to style my hair. You know how some women hire professional stylists to fix their hair prior to their weddings? Well, that does not happen in Casa Calloway. It's just me and my cheapo curling iron, doing the best we can.

Enzo prefers my hair down, but having it up is more traditional. Not that there are going to be tons of photos to post all over social media, but what if my parents want to take pictures? Or have pictures of me with them?

Maybe we will get a shot of the entire family together. A family photo. I never thought that would be possible.

I finally opt to leave my hair down, deciding that the appreciative look on Enzo's face will be worth it. I am careful not to scald myself with the curling iron, which tends to be a bit finicky, and after about half an hour, I have some pretty decent waves going on in my usually pin-straight blond hair. It will be straight again by the evening, but I only need it to last for the next three hours.

As I'm coming out of the bathroom, my phone is ringing where I last left it, which is on the coffee table in the living room. Much like the rest of the furniture in the apartment, we got our coffee table from the curb outside our building, and there's a book under the left leg to keep it from wobbling. I snatch my phone off the table just before the caller hangs up, and my heart sinks.

It's that same 718 number.

But on the plus side, Enzo isn't here to overhear the conversation. So I can feel free to give this guy a piece of my mind without anyone else catching wind of the fact that I am being threatened. I can dish it right back as well as I can take it.

I take a calming breath as I click on the green button to take the call. "Hello?"

"*Hello*, Millie." It's that same harsh whisper, like he's disguising his voice. "Or should I say *goodbye*?"

I roll my eyes. "Why would you say goodbye?"

"Because," he says, "today is going to be the last day of your life."

"Oh, is that so?" I shoot back, playing along for the moment.

"It's what you deserve," he taunts me. "After the lies you fed to my wife. You ruined my marriage, you bitch."

I was right—it's a disgruntled husband. I'm not even the tiniest bit surprised. I have helped a lot of women escape terrible marriages, and along the way, I have made some enemies. It goes with the territory. I wonder who this one is.

"And who is your wife?" I prompt him. I'll feel better if I know who this guy is.

"My wife was a whore," he spits out. "She was lucky to have me, but *you* convinced her otherwise."

God, this guy is a piece of work.

"I'm sure she's much better off without you," I say calmly. "And I suggest you accept it and try to grow from the experience." I add, "And also, leave me the hell alone."

"Grow from the experience!" he bursts out. "You have a lot of nerve, Millie Calloway! Women like you are the worst type of people. And I promise, you're going to pay for what you've done."

I would bet my life savings that this guy is all talk. Of course, it wouldn't be much of a risk since my bank account is mostly empty, especially after buying that blue dress that no longer fits me. "I don't think so."

"Think whatever you'd like," he says, "but I have a question for you, Millie."

"Fine." I grit my teeth, playing along for another second before I hang up on him and block his number. "What's your question?"

His voice takes on an amused edge. "Have you checked your coat closet since your boyfriend left this morning?"

FOUR

Have you checked your coat closet since your boyfriend left this morning?

My stomach flips as my gaze lifts to the small closet across the room from me, which contains our coats and boots. The door to the closet is closed. "What did you say?"

"Your coat closet," he repeats. "I've got a *great* view of you."

"You're lying," I choke out.

"I'm not, Millie." His voice is almost singsong. Teasing me. "But if you're so sure, why don't you check?"

Before he can taunt me further, I press the red button on my phone to end the call. I lower it from my ear with a trembling hand, wishing I had hung up a minute sooner. I was so certain this guy was harmless and just trying to scare me. All talk.

But how did he know Enzo left the apartment?

My eyes are pinned on the closet. The door is closed,

and there's no sign of light or movement underneath. Could someone possibly be hiding in there?

No, there couldn't be. We lock and deadbolt our door at night because we don't live in a great neighborhood. Actually, that's an understatement. Because our financial situation is rather tenuous at the moment and we're saving every penny for when the baby comes, the number one thing we were looking for in an apartment was "dirt cheap." The Bronx has some absolutely gorgeous suburban areas, but we live on what is possibly the most dangerous block in the whole borough. It's the kind of neighborhood where you don't venture out after dark. And it's the kind of neighborhood where you get a damn good lock.

Our lock is a damn good lock. It's a Grade 1 lock, which means it has resisted tests involving hammering, prying, sawing, picking, and even kicking. I suppose it's possible someone could get through our Super Lock, but it would have to involve at the very least a minor explosion. We would definitely hear it. Plus, Enzo would have grabbed his coat from the closet before leaving, and if someone were hiding in that tiny closet, he would have seen him.

Although…

I didn't deadbolt the door after Enzo left since I was in the bedroom when he took off. It seemed unnecessary; it's the middle of the day, and he said he'd be right back. We do have the best deadbolt on the market, but it has one fatal flaw: It doesn't work if I don't lock it.

Still, nobody could have gotten in. There wasn't enough time, and I almost certainly would have heard…

If you're so sure, why don't you check?

It's not possible. I would've heard him come in—I was right in the bathroom, curling my hair. I did have the noisy blow-dryer going at one point, but surely I still would've heard somebody breaking in. I'm 100 percent sure.

Okay, 99 percent sure.

My first thought is that I should get out of here. If there's any chance there's a man in the closet who wants to slit my throat, I need to hightail it ASAP.

But what if this is a trick? I'm safe behind the locks on the front door, but if I leave, I'll be a sitting duck. What if whoever is making the calls is right outside the door, and he's trying to scare me into leaving the safety of my apartment?

Of course, I *could* call 911. That's always an option. But I've now got less than three hours until my wedding. If I get the police involved, I may as well scratch "getting married" off my appointment book for today. A canceled wedding certainly won't do much to improve my parents' impression of me.

I need to talk to my fiancé. *Now.*

My hands are still trembling as I lift my phone and select Enzo's name from my list of contacts. The phone rings a couple of times before I hear his voice on the other line. Just the sound of his Italian accent is enough to soothe me.

"Millie!" His jubilance is a stark contrast to the tension I'm feeling. "We are in luck! My friend will have the dress ready in two hours. We will have time to get it before we have to be at city hall."

"Great." Any concern I had about the dress is completely overshadowed by my paralyzing fear of whatever is in the coat closet. "Are...are you almost home?"

"Soon. Five minutes. Maybe ten."

Ten minutes. A hell of a lot can happen in ten minutes.

"Everything is okay, Millie?" he asks me.

I should tell him what's going on. It's ridiculous not to. But my gut is still telling me that this man is messing with my head. And if that's the case, the only way he will win is if I let him ruin the most important day of my life. I don't want my wedding day to revolve around this asshole. It's bad enough that he's upset me, but if Enzo finds out, he will *not* let it go.

"Everything is fine," I manage. "Please…please come home soon."

"I will," he promises, although I can hear in his voice that he doesn't quite believe everything is fine. But since he's busy driving, he doesn't push me.

I end the call with my husband-to-be, and my gaze snaps back to the coat closet. There's nobody in there. There can't be. If there were, I would have *heard* him talking to me, wouldn't I? The closet is empty. I'm sure of it.

If you're so sure, why don't you check?

I could wait for Enzo to get home, but I don't want to. I want to call his bluff all on my own—nobody can intimidate Millie Calloway. There's nobody in that damn closet. He's trying to make me afraid, and I'm going to prove that I'm not.

Slowly, never taking my eyes off that coat closet, I back into the kitchen portion of our living room. For once, I'm grateful for how tiny our living space is. If there's any chance I'm going to check that closet, I need a weapon. I need to be ready for whatever is in there.

The knife block is inside the kitchen. I grab the biggest butcher knife we have—one that is certain not to miss even if I stab wildly. And then I creep across the living room, the knife gripped in my hand as I approach the coat closet.

I cross the room in only five steps. I am still clutching the butcher knife in my right hand, so tightly that my fingers are bloodless. If someone is in my closet and I kill him, it would be in self-defense. If it comes down to him versus me, I'll make sure I'm not the one lying on the floor in a pool of blood.

But it won't come down to that because there is nobody in this stupid closet. And I'm going to prove it right now.

I reach out my hand and close my fingers around the doorknob.

FIVE

Before I can turn the doorknob to the coat closet, keys jingle in the lock to the front door.

Oh my God, it's Enzo. He's *back*.

I release the knob, my shoulders sagging. I wanted to be brave, but I am so relieved I don't have to do this alone. It will be so much better now that he's here. Two against one is always better.

The door swings open, and my fiancé is standing in the doorway, minus one pale-blue wedding dress. He is wearing a coat over his jeans and T-shirt, and there is snow dotting the shoulders. He has a smile on his face, but it vanishes and his eyes go wide when he sees me.

"Millie," he gasps. "What are you doing with that knife?"

The fingers of my right hand are still closed around the handle of the butcher knife. I'm not quite sure how to explain this one without telling him everything. "I…I saw a mouse."

He cocks his head to the side. “I thought we use traps for that?”

I try to smile, but only one side of my lips moves upward. “I was improvising.”

“I see…” He closes and locks the front door behind us. The deadbolt is now secured in place, which is great, except the intruder *might already be inside.* “Where did the mouse go?”

“Uh…” I look over at the closet next to me. There are no sounds coming from inside or any indication that it contains anything but coats. “The closet. Do you, um, want to check?”

Enzo is still staring at the knife in my hand. “I think a broom might be better, yes?”

Except I am *not* letting go of this knife. Not until I am absolutely sure that nobody is inside our closet.

Sweetheart, I have been getting threatening calls all morning. I don’t think there is anyone hiding in our closet, but there might be. I’m getting a teensy bit worried, but I don’t want this to ruin the happiest day of our lives. So…could you just check the closet for me real quick?

The words are on the tip of my tongue, but I can’t bring myself to say them. I will tell him everything—tomorrow. Anyway, we’re going to be leaving for city hall soon. I won’t be alone at any point today. This will be fine.

Nobody is going to slit my throat in the immediate future.

Enzo strides over to the closet before I can stop him. My fingers tighten around the handle of the knife as his fingers close around the knob. As he wrenches the door open he lets out a gasp. I raise the blade of the knife, ready to strike.

"Millie," he says, "why do you have so many boots?"

What?

He crouches down and pulls out a pair of knee-high leather boots. He holds them up accusingly. "You have no dresses, but you have five kinds of boots? Why is this?"

"I like boots," I admit weakly. "And those were on sale."

He shakes his head. "Well, I do not see a mouse. So you can lower your weapon."

I lower the knife, but I'm not quite ready to let go of it. I do feel vindicated though. I knew that asshole on the phone wasn't in my closet. I mean, I was pretty sure.

"By the way," he says as he tosses my shoes back in the closet, "I thought of another name as I was giving my friend your dress."

"Oh yeah?"

"Violet."

I raise my eyebrows. "My dress is *blue*, you know."

"Yes, but Blue is not a good name for a girl."

"I don't know. I'm not really feeling Violet. How about Cyan?"

He frowns the way he always does when somebody says a word in English that he doesn't know. "What is a Cyan?"

"It's a color. Sort of a mix between green and blue."

"I thought it was a poison used to kill people."

"That's cyanide."

"Same thing." His gaze drops to the knife still clutched in my right hand. "Do you want to put the knife away now, Millie? I think we are safe from the mouse."

Actually, I'd like to hold on to the knife, but I can't

spend my wedding day walking around with a knife in my hand. So very reluctantly, I return to the kitchen and put it back in the block.

I've got Mace in my purse, after all.

SIX

Enzo drives into Manhattan so I don't have to wade through the accumulating snow in my pumps ("Is this not what all the boots are for, Millie?"), and he manages to find a parking spot that isn't metered. I can just imagine Enzo having to duck out during the ceremony to feed a meter every fifteen minutes, so I'm grateful for the good parking. My luck is holding out.

Enzo's tailor friend is going to meet us in Manhattan, which is where he has his shop. I dress in a nice skirt and blouse, just in case somehow the adjustments are unsuccessful, which seems like a distinct possibility. Unfortunately, my outfit doesn't seem like something a person would wear to get married, and it also contains no blue whatsoever. During the drive to Manhattan, I googled *does the dollar store sell dresses?* (Apparently, they do sell "clothing and apparel.")

We locate a cafe next to where we parked. We get a table inside, near the window so I can watch the snowflakes that continue to fall. I'm too nervous to eat, so all I get is a cup of coffee. How am I supposed to eat a muffin when I'm going to get married *in an hour*? I especially don't understand how Enzo could get a full breakfast with an omelet and hash browns.

"If you spill any food on that shirt, I am going to kill you," I inform him.

Enzo looks up at me and grins. He is devastatingly handsome in the (thanks to me) crisp white shirt he is wearing, as well as a black jacket and slacks. He looks so good that our waitress has been flirting with him shamelessly, even though his future wife is literally sitting across from him, drumming her fingers against the table.

"I would never," he says. "I am careful."

I check my watch restlessly and then shift my gaze back out the window. "Isn't your friend supposed to be here by now? We're never going to make it in time."

"Relax. We have a whole hour."

"If I don't get the dress, I won't have my something blue *or* my something new."

"Your earrings are new," he points out.

I'm impressed that he recognized I've never worn them before, but the shimmery diamond earrings hanging from my earlobes are neither blue nor new. "These are *borrowed*," I explain patiently. A former client of mine lent them to me for the occasion. She tried to give them to me, but I told her that they had to be borrowed.

Enzo nods in understanding, even though I'm pretty sure he is just humoring me. "There is a gift shop next door. We can buy you a blue key chain with your name on it."

"There are no Millie key chains. Believe me—I've checked. I don't have a key chain kind of name."

"Me either," he says. "Maybe your mother will give you something blue?"

"My mother is already giving me something old," I say. "A necklace. Besides, it's already going to be tense when my parents show up, without me demanding blue items."

Enzo shovels a bite of eggs into his mouth. "Do not worry. You are their daughter. They love you."

"Uh-huh." I take a drink of my coffee, although the caffeine might be making my nerves worse. Really, I need a shot of whiskey, but I don't think this cafe sells alcohol. "They love me so much that I haven't seen them in fifteen years."

"Of course they love you," he says again, more firmly. The right side of his lips twists up. "And of course, you know they will love *me*."

Despite everything, I have to laugh. My mother, at least, will be enamored of Enzo. I can't wait for her to meet him. "You better charm the pants off them."

"Always."

I take another sip of my coffee. It took me the entire drive from the Bronx to Manhattan to stop shaking after the debacle with the coat closet. During the drive, I got another call from that 718 number, but this time I wisely declined. I'll fill Enzo in on the details later, but not today. This day is already stressful enough without dealing with a death threat, which I still don't think is credible. I know when a man is just trying to scare me.

I thought about blocking the number, but then I decided it was possible the guy would be dumb enough to leave a message, and it would be something I could play for Enzo later. Or it could be useful to show to the police if it came down to that, but I doubt it ever will.

Although, I admit, I'm a little unsettled about the fact that the man knew Enzo had left the apartment. It's the one thing that makes me concerned that these aren't just empty threats.

Enzo stuffs a few chunks of fried potato into his mouth. "Are you sure you don't want any?"

"Definitely not."

"You need to eat. You are making another person."

I shake my head no. "I'm too nervous to eat."

"Why are you nervous? You are not having the… double thoughts?"

I stare at him in confusion for a moment before I realize what he's trying to say. "*Second* thoughts?"

"Yes," he says, nodding vigorously. "You are not having the second thoughts, right?"

He says it in a teasing tone, but there's an undercurrent of worry in his voice. I don't know why though. How could he possibly think I wouldn't want to marry him? Even if I wasn't pregnant with his child, I'd want to marry him.

"No second thoughts," I assure him. "It's just…a lot. It's scary getting married, isn't it?"

"Why scary? This is not scary." He puts down his fork to look into my eyes, something that still makes my whole body tingle. "All I ever wanted is to spend the rest of my life with you. We are just making it in writing now." He reaches for my hands, and when I give them to him, he laces his fingers into mine. "I can't wait for you to be my wife."

It's the first thing he has said that has calmed me down entirely. I squeeze his hands back, and once again, I think to myself, *I am lucky.* We are going to have a great day today. The best of our lives.

And that's when, through the snowflakes still falling outside the window of the cafe, I see the gaunt man staring at us, a murderous glint in his eyes.

SEVEN

That's him.

The man staring at us through the window of the cafe is wearing a trench coat that is damp from the snow, his hands shoved deep into his pockets. He is older than I expected him to be—possibly in his sixties—with hollowed eyes, which bore straight into me. His lips twist into a sneer that turns my blood to ice.

I had been hoping to hide those threatening calls from Enzo, but now that the man has shown up in person with a menacing expression on his face, I have to say something. I have no choice. At least, if I don't want to be *murdered* on my wedding day.

And now the man has entered the cafe. He is standing less than ten feet away from us. He's got a paper bag in his right hand that he is clutching so tightly that all the tendons stand out. I watch in horror as he reaches into the bag.

Oh God.

"Enzo," I whisper urgently. "Do you see that man over there?"

Enzo swivels his head to look at the entrance to the cafe. I expect his eyes to darken the way they always do when he perceives a threat. So I'm not prepared for the sudden smile that lights his face as he jumps to his feet.

"Giuseppe!" he cries.

Giuseppe?

To my utter shock, Enzo rushes across the cafe and then embraces the man in the trench coat. What follows is a string of rapid Italian. I can only make out two words, one of which is Millie and the other is *pazza*, which I'm becoming more and more convinced is not complimentary.

After about a minute of conversation, Enzo pulls the older man over to our table. "Millie," he says, "this is my good friend, Giuseppe."

"*Buongiorno*, Millie," the man says in heavily accented English. This is most definitely *not* the man from the phone.

"Hello," I say politely. "It's very nice to meet you."

"Giuseppe," Enzo says, "is a tailor."

Giuseppe reaches into the paper bag and pulls out my pale-blue dress. "For you, *mia cara*."

He did it. He managed to get it altered in time for the wedding. It's a wedding-day miracle. Tears form in my eyes as I clutch my dress in both hands. "Thank you so much, Giuseppe."

He beams at me. "You are welcome. But please, try it on. I want to make sure it fits."

Thankfully, the cafe has a bathroom in the back where I can change. I excuse myself from the table and hurry down a long, dimly lit hallway to get to the single-person restroom. There's no indication whether it's vacant or not, but I knock several times, and when someone doesn't yell that the room is occupied, I try the knob and find it empty. This isn't exactly where I hoped to be changing into my wedding dress, but I'm just grateful that I didn't have to change in the middle of the cafe or at some McDonald's.

I step out of my skirt and blouse, being careful not to let them fall on the floor or, God forbid, inside the toilet. The restroom is clean, at least, which is more than I can say for a lot of restrooms in New York City restaurants. I slip the dress on over my head, and the blue fabric drapes over the curve of my belly and hips. It seems to fit well enough, but the real test is whether it zips in the back.

I position my hands behind me, locating the zipper with my fingers. Here we go—moment of truth.

I tug on the zipper, and to my utter relief, it slides up easily. It doesn't fit quite the same way it did before, and my belly does have a somewhat noticeable bulge, but that's fine. I'm not ashamed of the baby growing inside me. I think the dress looks fantastic, although it's hard to tell since all I've got is a vanity mirror.

Enzo solved the problem, just like he promised he would. I've got a perfect dress, as well as something new and something blue.

My phone rings inside my purse, which is balanced on the edge of the sink. I assume it's Enzo, asking if the dress fits, so I answer the phone without thinking about it. It's only when I hear the low, menacing voice on the other end of the line that I realize my mistake—I should have blocked the number earlier.

"Nice dress," that now-familiar voice rasps into my ear. "I can't wait to see how it looks with your blood spilled all over it."

I grip the phone in my right hand, too surprised to speak.

"Don't blue and red make purple?" he asks in a mock innocent voice. "You would look great in purple, Millie."

"You need to stay away from me," I croak. "You have no idea who you're dealing with."

"I'd love to find out…"

"Too bad."

"Oh, I think I will," he says. "After all, I'm right on the other side of the bathroom door."

And then the doorknob starts to turn.

EIGHT

I locked it. Of course I locked it.

Like any sane person, the first thing I did when I went into the public restroom was lock the door so nobody else could get in. But the lock is considerably less sophisticated than the deadbolt on the door to our apartment. It's one of those hook-and-eye locks, which looks like it'll come loose with one good rattle. The knob turns counterclockwise, and I step back, pressing myself against the white tile wall of the bathroom, as whoever is trying to get inside shakes the door.

My purse. It's on the edge of the sink, and I've got my can of Mace inside. If this asshole wants to hurt me, I'm going to put up a hell of a fight.

I grab my purse and rifle around inside. I feel for the reassuring bottle that I keep with me at all times. But to my frustration, I can't seem to find it. Where is my Mace?

Then I remember. I was talking to a friend in one of

my classes last week, and she mentioned she was going out with a new guy she met on some dating app. I got bad vibes when she said he wouldn't give her his phone number and would only message through the app, but when she insisted on going on the date anyway, I forced her to take my bottle of Mace. Just in case.

She survived the date. (The guy turned out to be a jerk, but not dangerous.) But I told her to keep the Mace, figuring I'd get another bottle. Then I forgot.

Shit. What am I going to do?

Before I can descend into panic, a voice from behind the door calls out: "Hello? Anyone in there?"

It's a female voice. Definitely not the person on the phone. It's just a woman who wants to use the ladies' room.

That man is not on the other side of the door.

"Just a minute!" I call out.

Okay, he was full of shit *yet again*, at least about being behind the bathroom door. But at the same time, that call was incredibly disturbing. He knew about the blue dress. He knew I was in the bathroom. He is watching me.

He's here.

I grab my purse and the clothes I had been wearing, and I come out of the bathroom. The woman standing on the other side of the door flashes me an apologetic smile, but I'm too upset to even return it. As much as I don't want to, I have to tell Enzo what's going on. He needs to know I am being threatened, and that this is a credible threat. We need to figure out together how to handle it.

When I get back into the dining area, Enzo is still deep in conversation with his friend. But when he sees me, he rises to his feet and straightens his tie. A smile lights his face.

"Millie," he says in a slightly breathless voice. "You look… You are so beautiful."

A man has been threatening me all day. He told me he was going to cut my throat. He's watching me.

I've got to tell Enzo what's going on, but the words die on my lips when his eyes become moist. "You have made me such a happy man," he manages. "I am so lucky you will be my wife."

He said he wants to see my blood spill all over my dress.

"I love you so much." He wraps his arms around me, making me feel safe and loved in a way I haven't felt in a very, very long time with anyone besides Enzo Accardi. "This is the best day of my life."

Oh hell.

I can't tell him right now. I won't let that asshole destroy our wedding day.

It will be fine. I'll just keep my eyes peeled, Mace or no Mace.

But as I'm pulling away from Enzo's embrace, out of the corner of my eye, I catch sight of a stout man sitting on the far side of the cafe, nursing a cup of coffee. The man is dressed in an ill-fitting suit and tie, and his head is shaved so that his white, egg-shaped scalp gleams in the overhead light. He is watching me and Enzo, an unreadable expression on his face.

Could that be the man who has been threatening me?

His eyes meet mine for a split second, and then he looks away, suddenly absorbed in something on his phone. He doesn't look up again.

It's entirely possible I'm imagining things, but my gut tells me there was recognition in that man's eyes when he looked at me. And my gut is rarely wrong.

NINE

Our appointment to get married is at eleven thirty.

The timing is perfect. We will get married, and then afterward, Enzo and I will have lunch with my parents at a nice restaurant downtown. He will get to know them properly, and we will be on our way to being a real family. I am a perfect combination of nervous and excited. I am nervicited.

God, I'm so nervous that I'm making up words now.

We are supposed to meet my parents in front of the steps of city hall on Worth Street at ten past eleven. We make it there with a few minutes to spare, which is a good thing because my mother is a stickler for punctuality. When I was a kid, she would get so mad at me if I was late for anything—and there were *no* excuses. When I was in middle school, I had to bring a friend to the emergency room because she tripped on our way home and split her forehead open so badly that it wouldn't stop bleeding, and I *still* got grounded for a month for being fifteen minutes late for my scheduled piano lesson. Since we're restarting our relationship, I want to make sure to put my best foot forward.

The snow has stopped falling, but there's still a sprinkle of white powder on the ground. In about half an hour, all the snow will have turned into gray (or worse, yellow) slush, but for the moment, it's pretty. I hug my peacock-green coat to my chest for warmth although the coldest part of me is my ears, which could be in danger of frostbite if we don't go inside soon.

Enzo, who is wearing a black beanie without the slightest concern for his hair, notices me cupping my ears to keep them warm, although all that seems to do is make my fingers cold. "Do you want my hat?" he offers.

Is he out of his ever-loving *mind*? "Do you know how long it took to get my hair to look this way?"

"It looks the same way it always does." A second after the words leave his mouth, he recognizes his mistake and quickly adds, "Always beautiful."

Nice save, Enzo.

"I do not want you to be cold," he says. "You are making heat for two now."

I roll my eyes. "It's fine. My parents will be here soon. I only need to keep warm a little longer."

When I mention my parents, I instinctively touch my neckline. I didn't wear a necklace because I'm waiting for my mother's heirloom. If I wore anything else, she'd complain it would outshine the jewelry she gave me.

"Relax," Enzo says. "Do not worry so much. Everything will be fine."

"You don't know my parents." I curl a flattened

tendril of hair with my finger. "They need everything to be perfect. If everything isn't perfect, then…"

"So we will be perfect." He flashes me a toothy grin. "Yes?"

I check my watch. "Where are they anyway? How come they're so late?"

"So late? It is 11:12. Two minutes late."

"That's extremely late for my parents, believe me."

I crane my neck, looking down the street to see if they're coming. I don't see my parents, but my attention is distracted by another person who is standing by the steps to city hall. I squint and blink my eyes, not sure if I'm seeing right.

It's the bald-headed man from the cafe. The one who I thought was staring at me. He's got his phone to his ear, and once again, he's looking in my direction.

It could be a coincidence, but somehow, I don't think so. Especially when he looks up at me then quickly looks away again when our eyes meet. I consider walking over there to get a closer look or even confront him, but before I can, my phone starts ringing.

Is that him? He's got his phone in his hand, so it certainly could be. Although if he called me now, it would be very clear he's the one making the calls.

But maybe he wants me to know.

I fumble with my purse, practically dropping it in the snow. I hold my breath when I pull my phone out of the purse, expecting to see that 718 number again, so it's a relief when I see the name "Mom" flashing on the screen—she must have gotten caught in traffic and is calling to apologize. I take the call.

"Mom?" I say.

There's a long pause on the other end of the line. I listen for sounds of traffic in the background but hear nothing. "Hello, Millie."

"Are you almost here?"

Another long pause. "No."

"But our appointment is in less than twenty minutes!"

"Millie..." There's yet another pause, and this one seems to last an eternity. "Your father and I aren't coming."

"*What?*"

Enzo's dark eyebrows shoot up at the sputtered word. "What's wrong?" he mouths, but I shake my head. Instead, he dips his head close to mine so that he can hear what my mother is saying.

"I'm sorry," she says, as if that helps even the tiniest bit.

"But...why aren't you coming?"

I wait for news of a terrible accident on the highway that prevented them from making it to the wedding of their only child. Maybe my father fell and broke his hip. Maybe an earthquake created a deep crater between their house and city hall.

"We never should have agreed to come in the first place," she says in that maddeningly logical voice that I used to hate. I forgot how much she used to get on my nerves. "We had hoped that everything you went through had changed you. But after your father and I discussed it, we realized you're just as much of a mess as you always were. I mean, the only reason you're getting married in the first place is because you got yourself knocked up."

She's not wrong, but still... "It happens, Mother."

"And now you're marrying…who?" She gives a snort of derision. "Some blue-collar immigrant in search of a green card?"

Enzo jerks his head away from the phone, looking affronted. "I *have* a green card!"

I wave my hand at him, knowing this objection won't help. "You told me you were coming. You said that you wanted to be a part of my life and a part of your granddaughter's life."

"I'm sorry," she says again, and I want to reach through the phone and throttle her. "I just can't bear to watch you raise a girl that turns out the same way you did."

I am speechless.

Enzo takes the opportunity to wrench the phone from my hands. Before I can stop him, he is speaking sharply to my mother. I want to tell him not to bother, that once my mother has made up her mind, there's no changing it back. But Enzo has that look in his eyes, and I can tell he needs to say his piece.

"Mrs. Calloway," he says. He's respectful—I'll give him that. "I want you to know that I love your daughter very much, and I will take very good care of her and our child. I already have a green card, and I do not want to marry her for that reason. I want to marry her because I *love* her and I want to spend the rest of my life with her. She loves you also, and it meant so much to her that you were coming. If there is any way you could be here, if not for the ceremony, then…"

There is a long pause while he listens to whatever my mother is saying to him. His olive skin rarely shows signs of his emotions, but now his face turns red. "No," he says in a low voice that is simmering with rage, "she does not *need* to change because there was never anything wrong with her in the first place." Another tense pause and his voice drops. "No, I do not believe I am making a mistake."

He listens for another several seconds, and then finally, he shakes his head. "You do not know your daughter at all," he says in a voice that is simultaneously angry and sad. "I hope someday you will realize the terrible mistake you have made. But for now, we do not want you here or in our lives."

I stare at him as he ends the call and wordlessly hands my phone back to me. I give him a second as he struggles to maintain his composure.

"What did she say?" I ask, even though I'm not sure I want to know.

"You are better off without them" is all he says.

He won't even tell me. That's fine though. I got the gist of it.

Wow. I can't believe this is happening. My parents aren't coming to my wedding. They have left their only child all alone on her wedding day.

"We don't have a witness anymore," I say, my voice cracking embarrassingly on the words.

"We'll find one," he promises. "It is a whole city hall. Lots of people."

"And…and I don't have my something old anymore…"

My head is spinning. This was supposed to be the best day of my life, but it's been one tragedy after another. Is this a sign that Enzo and I are not meant to be? Or maybe it's just that this morning, I dared to think of myself as lucky. How could I have been so stupid? I'm not lucky—I'm *never* lucky! I am the unluckiest person in the entire world.

And just to top it all off, that bald man is still staring at me.

I stare back in his direction. This time, he doesn't look away. He glares right back at me with venom in his eyes. This is clearly him—the man who has been threatening to cut my throat. This is the man who has been telling me that he will kill me on my wedding day.

Well, I have had enough.

Before I can stop myself, I stride across the snow-coated sidewalk in the direction of the bald man, not caring about my wholly inappropriate footwear. My hands clench into fists, and my heart slams in my chest.

This is going to end right now.

TEN

It takes me about two seconds to walk across the sidewalk to where the bald man is standing. Enzo is hurrying after me, calling my name. On the plus side, I have entirely forgotten about the evolving frostbite in my ears.

"Millie!" he cries. "Please! I love you. Your parents do not matter!"

But I don't stop until I am right in front of the man in the dark suit. Close enough that I can stick my finger in his face. I want him to know that I'm not afraid of him. I don't care how many times he calls me or what threats he hisses into the phone. He will not intimidate me.

I'm Millie freaking Calloway, and I'm not afraid of *anyone*.

"Listen to me, you piece of shit!" I spit out at him. "I know who you are!"

His eyes widen, and I'm surprised by the bright-blue color. "You are Millie Calloway, aren't you?"

"Damn straight!" I grit my teeth. "And I just want you to know that whatever I did, I did for the right reason. And if you think you can threaten me, you better think again! I am a lot tougher than you think I am, buddy."

The bald man blinks rapidly. "Yes, I know you're tough. You saved my sister's life."

I freeze, mid-diatribe. That is not what I expected him to say at all. "I…what?"

The man's lips twitch into a shy smile as he squeezes his hands together. "I'm so glad I finally get to meet you." His eyelashes flutter again—a nervous tic. "My name is Paul. My sister… Her name is Diana Widmayer… Dee… And she was in a terrible marriage. Her husband would have killed her for sure, and he had buddies on the police force. Dee was trapped. You helped her get away." His eyes fill with moisture, and a single tear escapes from his left eye. "You saved my sister's life. We owe you everything."

Dee Widmayer. Of course. I remember her from about a year ago. I remember the bruises all over her arms and legs and back, where her husband thought nobody would see them. "Is Dee doing okay?"

"She is. Thanks to you." He reaches out to clasp my hand in both of his. "When I saw you, I just had to tell you how much what you did meant to us. If there's anything you ever need…anything I could do for you…"

Okay, I believe this guy isn't the one who has been threatening me on the phone. Unless he is an Oscar-winning actor, his gratitude is genuine. Those tears are real and on the brink of spilling over.

"You don't owe me anything," I blurt out. "I'm just glad your sister is okay."

"Actually..." Enzo clears his throat, inserting himself into our little moment. "There is one favor you can do for us."

Paul's eyes light up. "Of course! Like I said, anything you want."

"Millie and I are about to get married," Enzo explains, "and it turns out we have no witness. Do you think you could...?"

Paul beams. "It would be my honor!"

Enzo winks at me. "See? I told you we would find a witness. And as for the something old..." He looks over at Paul, who is eagerly straightening his tie in anticipation of the ceremony. It's sort of adorable. "Would you excuse us for a moment?"

Enzo leads me away from the other man, who looks so harmless right now, it seems embarrassing that I could have thought he was the threatening caller. Enzo stops when we are out of earshot and flashes me a conspiratorial smile.

"I know you were hoping for your mother's necklace," he says, "but I want to give you something instead that belongs to me. It's something that means a lot to me, and it would mean so much to me if you would hold on to it during the ceremony."

I frown at him. "What is it?"

Enzo digs around in his pocket for several seconds, which is long enough for me to start to worry. He always carries this old pocket knife his father gave him with his initials engraved on it—does he want *that* to be my "something old"? I wouldn't be entirely surprised if he whipped that out, but I am *not* carrying a knife during my wedding ceremony. Plus, they have metal detectors at city hall.

But instead, he pulls out a small turquoise item. He holds it out in his palm, and I realize that it's a butterfly pin.

"This belonged to Antonia." His voice breaks the way it often does when he says his sister's name. It's because of Antonia and what her husband did to her that Enzo and I are together in the first place. "My mother gave it to her as a little girl, and I found it in her jewelry box after she was killed. I carry it around always to remind me of her. And…I want you to hold on to it during the ceremony."

"Enzo…"

"Please."

I don't protest again. He reaches out to pin the tiny butterfly to the fabric covering my shoulder. The color suits the dress perfectly, as if I had picked it out to match.

"There," he says. "Now you have something old."

"Thank you," I breathe.

"So." He lifts his dark eyes to meet mine. "We may get married now?"

I allow a smile to touch my lips. "We may."

ELEVEN

Ten minutes later, we are waiting in city hall for our number to be called.

Yes, this is how getting married works at city hall. You take a number and sit in a plastic chair, waiting for them to call you. I try not to let it bother me that getting married so closely resembles getting a sandwich at the deli. On the plus side, my ears are warm.

Our number is twenty-six, and they have just called twenty-three. Based on how quickly the last few numbers went by, I expect we will be called in the next five minutes. In another fifteen minutes, Enzo Accardi will officially be my husband.

"TWENTY-FOUR!" a voice calls out.

"Last chance to change your mind," Enzo teases me.

I open my mouth to sass him back, but then something stops me. A slight fluttering in my belly. It almost feels like an air bubble rising up from my insides and poking me. I clutch my abdomen, waiting to see if I feel it again.

And then there it is. Another little flutter.

Enzo's brow lowers. "Are you okay?"

"I think…" I take a deep breath. "The baby just kicked me."

"Really?" He rests his own hand on the slight swell of my belly. "I don't feel anything."

"TWENTY-FIVE!"

Another couple rises to their feet, disappearing down a hallway. It's like getting closer in line to a ride that you're excited about taking. Except you know the ride also has some massive drop and a bit of upside-down stuff, so you're simultaneously terrified.

I feel that fluttering again, but Enzo just shakes his head. He can't feel her yet. For now, her kicks are just for me.

"You'll feel her when she gets bigger," I promise him.

Paul, who is sitting across from us, speaks up: "I remember feeling my wife's belly when she was pregnant with our son. That kid kicked all the time! No wonder he likes soccer so much."

Enzo keeps his hand pressed against my abdomen. "I will feel little Harriet soon enough."

"Harriet?" I shake my head emphatically. "I don't think so."

"What about Paula?" Paul suggests.

"TWENTY-SIX!"

"That's us," Enzo murmurs in my ear.

He reaches for my hand, and we get to our feet like the couples before us did, and Paul follows close behind. I am trembling as we follow the city hall employee down a hallway until we reach the chapel, which really is more like a conference room, although there is a podium at the front. When I was a child, I always imagined I would get married in a church in front of a priest. But here, in front of a judge, is just as good.

Because I'm here with the man that I love.

It's a standard courthouse wedding ceremony, which is supposed to average no more than two minutes, so it wasn't like we could write our own vows or anything like that. But the judge at the front has kind eyes, and he smiles at us as he tells us to join hands.

"You're shaking," Enzo whispers to me, a smile playing on his lips.

"I'm excited."

I *am* shaking, but it's not the same way I was shaking when I thought there was an intruder in my closet this morning. I'm shaking because this is the most amazing thing that has ever happened to me, although that may move to second place when our daughter is born.

"We are gathered here today," the judge begins, "in the presence of witnesses for the purpose of uniting in matrimony Wilhelmina Calloway and Enzo Accardi..."

The judge talks about how the contract of marriage is solemn and not one to enter into lightly. That we are pledging ourselves to each other for a lifetime. Enzo is nodding along with what the judge is saying, taking it all so seriously.

I'm glad it's you, I think to myself. For once, I made the right decision.

"Do you, Wilhelmina Calloway," the judge says, "take Enzo Accardi to be your lawful wedded husband? To have and to hold from this day forward, for better or for worse, for richer or poorer, in sickness and in health, to love and to cherish as long as you both shall live?"

"I do," I croak.

"Do you, Enzo Accardi," he continues, "take Wilhelmina Calloway to be your lawful wedded wife? To have and to hold from this day forward, for better or for worse, for richer or poorer, in sickness and in health, to love and to cherish as long as you both shall live?"

"That is not long enough," he says softly. "But yes. Yes, I do."

The next thing we do is exchange rings—simple gold bands that we bought online. After the debacle with my wedding dress this morning, I am frightened the ring won't fit my finger anymore. I hold my breath, expecting the worst, but thankfully, it slides right into place. *I thee wed*.

"You have joined yourselves in solemn matrimony," the judge says. "Love is truly the greatest gift we are given to share, and never take the other for granted, for you are destined to spend the rest of your lives joined together. And now, by virtue of the authority vested in me by the State of New York as Deputy Marriage Commissioner, I now pronounce you husband and wife for life." He pauses. "You may kiss."

Okay, finally—the good part.

Enzo—*my husband!*—leans in to give me a kiss that is very courthouse inappropriate, but I don't care. I can almost imagine the kind-faced judge giving us a side-eye, and for once, I'm sort of glad my parents aren't here to witness it. But we have earned this kiss. We have earned this life together.

And I will live happily ever after with my husband.

EPILOGUE

ENZO

Millie and I are married. This is the greatest day of my life.

I have had many bad days. Too many to count. I have watched my sister murdered. I was with both my parents at their deathbeds. There are so many days I wish to erase from my memory. But not this day. This day is perfect.

Nothing will ruin it for us.

Millie—*my wife!*—is still shaking as we hold hands leaving the chapel. She can't stop smiling, and all I can think is that I want to get her home—*now*. I am glad I have my car because I do not want to wait for the subway. She loves that blue dress, but it takes everything I have not to rip it off her. I almost can't breathe when I think about it.

"What are you thinking?" she says to me.

Is she kidding with me? "You *know* what I am thinking."

She grins even wider. I am sorry for what her parents did to her and for the awful things they said to me, warning me not to marry this wonderful woman because she is "dangerous." They said such terrible things. I will never, ever repeat those words to my wife for the rest of our lives.

Millie will hurt you. She can't control herself. She may cost you your life someday.

They do not know my Millie at all. They do not deserve to be part of our family.

"So." Millie squeezes my hand. "Should we go home?"

Something catches my attention at the side of the room. My eyes snap up for a split second, but before she can notice, I focus my gaze back on Millie. I need to pretend I did not see what I just saw, but I also need to take care of it. This is more urgent than anything we will do in the bedroom. There is a lifetime for that.

"Just a minute," I tell her. "I need to use the bathroom."

Millie says she needs to do the same, so we part ways. I disappear into the men's room, which is small and seems empty except for a thin man in his forties with dark-brown hair wearing a T-shirt and jeans, who is using the urinal. Very quickly, I check under all the stalls, but I do not see signs that anyone else is in here. We are alone, this man and me.

So I return to the restroom door and turn the lock.

The thin man zips up his fly and washes his hands at the sink. I allow him a moment to finish rinsing off the soap before I come up behind him, grabbing him by the collar with my left fist. I then slam him against the bathroom wall so hard that his head makes a resounding *clunk*.

The man's brown eyes widen with surprise and fear. He tries to claw at my hand holding his collar, but it is a sad attempt. This scrawny man has no chance of loosening my grip. I will not release him until I am done.

"What are you doing?" he gasps.

"I saw you," I say in a low, even voice. I do not want him to know how angry I am. I want to rip him limb from limb, but I cannot do that. Not here or now. "I saw you following us since we were at the cafe."

"I…I wasn't…"

"*Do not lie*." I draw back my right hand and slam it into his nose. Bone crunches underneath my fist. "Tell me why you were following us."

Blood spills from the man's nostrils, and he grabs his nose to staunch the flow. "I didn't…"

"Next I break your fingers."

"Okay!" The man's lips tremble in fear. "Your girlfriend convinced my wife to leave me and take my kids too. Millie helped her, and…and she ruined my life. You know how much child support is costing me? That bitch took me for *everything*. Your girlfriend deserves to *pay*."

"That is not my girlfriend—that is my wife." It's the first time I have said those words out loud. I am sorry it has to be to this dirtbag. "I do not know what Millie did, but your wife is better off without you." I lower my voice. "And if you do not stay away from my wife, I swear to God that I will break every single bone in your body. *Capisci?*"

The man gapes at me. "But she—"

"*Every bone in your body*," I repeat, "if you so much

as breathe on Millie Accardi ever again. *Do you understand me?*"

"Yes," he manages. "Yes…I…Yes, I'll stay away."

"Do you promise?"

"Yes. I promise!"

"Good." I level my gaze at him. "Because I will keep my promise too. If you go anywhere near her, I will break every bone in your body, one by one. And if you hurt her…" I pause just long enough for the fear to flicker in his eyes. "I will kill you."

With those words, I slam him hard against the bathroom wall again, this time hard enough to knock him out. His body goes limp, and I let him fall to the floor.

The next thing I do is check his back pocket. It contains his wallet. I remove his driver's license, which has his name and address, and I keep that because I want him to know I have it. I toss the wallet on the floor with the rest of his money and credit cards. If someone else takes it, that is not my problem. It is less than what he deserves.

He is already waking up, blinking his unfocused eyes as he groans with pain. I did not hit him hard enough that he will not remember our conversation. But I will pay him a visit as a reminder. I have his home address now.

Last, I wash the blood off my knuckles at the sink. I do not want Millie to know what I have just done. I cannot upset her—it has already been a difficult day for her without knowing a man has been following us all morning. I have taken care of it. I will not let this ruin our wedding day.

I will protect her. As long as I live and breathe, nobody will ever hurt her or our children.

When I get out of the bathroom, Millie is waiting for me. She smiles at me. "You took a long time in there! You're usually so much faster than me in the bathroom."

It would not do to tell her I took a little longer because I had to break a man's nose and threaten his life. "I am sorry."

"By the way..." She fingers my sister's pin on her chest. I truly believe part of my sister's spirit is in that butterfly pin, and because Millie wore it, Antonia was here with us today. I *felt* her presence, and it made me smile. "I was thinking a little more about baby names."

Millie never likes my ideas for names, although I am mostly joking in my suggestions. It is still early, and we have much time to decide. "Oh yes?"

"Yes." She nods. "I thought...maybe we could name our daughter after Antonia?"

I suck in a breath. I would love to honor my sister, but I also worry that giving her the same name will be too much. I can barely say her name without feeling a deep sadness that she left us much too young.

"Not the same exact name," Millie quickly amends, reading my face, "but something similar. To honor her. Like...Allison. Or Ada."

"Yes." I put my arms around my wife, drawing her close. "I like that."

And then I go home with my wife and unborn child, leaving the man who threatened us in a puddle of his own blood on the men's room floor.

THE END

Read on for a sneak peek of Freida's next thriller, *The Divorce.*

PROLOGUE

When the police arrive, how will I explain the dead bodies in the house?

Only one dead body would be easier to explain. People die, after all—circle of life, etc., etc. But more than one becomes trickier. Not that I have a lot of experience with it, but it's just common sense. One person can die by accident. Multiple deaths...well, the police start to think about things like *murder*.

Furthermore, it will be very difficult to explain other things to the police. Like what happened to those dead bodies *before* they died. I expect a lot of raised eyebrows. Possibly handcuffs.

Speaking of which, those sirens are getting awfully loud. They'll be here any second.

A gust of wind blows the stench of scorched flesh into my nostrils. Every molecule in my body is screaming at me to make a run for it while I still can. I've got a tiny window of time before the police arrive. I could hop in my car and take off. The nosy neighbor who called 911 in the first place might be able to point them in the right general direction, but nothing more. I could go somewhere that they will never, ever find me. I could turn into a ghost.

But it will be hard to disappear completely. Because wherever I go, I won't be alone. After all, it's not like I did any of this for myself. I did it all for *him*.

The sirens are growing louder by the second. I have less than a minute before they arrive. If there was ever a window to disappear, I have missed it. Very soon, everyone will find out the unthinkable thing that happened in this house. And when they do, there will be questions to answer.

The police car arrives first, screeching to a halt crookedly along the curb. As the officer climbs out of the driver's seat, I raise my hands high in the air where he can see them.

My life is about to change forever.

CHAPTER 1

NAOMI

My first clue that something is wrong is that my garage door won't open.

We have one of those "intelligent" garage doors that senses my Lexus when I pull into the driveway, rolling up the door at the exact moment to prevent collision with my front fender. The garage door is a feature my husband proudly showed me when we moved into this house, joking that it was smarter than I am, and in all the years I've lived here, it's never proven him wrong.

Until today.

I throw my Lexus into Park and stare at the garage door as if it's a puzzle I have to solve. There's a way to open it manually—I'm sure of it. I have a distinct memory of Jeremy telling me that if it didn't open automatically, all I would have to do is—

"Mommy?" Teddy's babyish voice pipes up from the back seat. "Is the door broken?"

I turn to look at my son, still wearing his white

uniform from the karate class I just picked him up from. He is strapped into a car seat in the back, even though at five years old, he's getting a little big to be sitting in one. He looks almost comically big for it, but I read that in the case of a rollover accident, there is nothing safer. And our pediatrician recommended the car seat until age six, so I ignore the eye rolls from some of the other women at kindergarten pickup.

"I don't think so," I say.

"Then why won't it open?"

Excellent question.

I glance over at the house, where the lights are on inside, signaling that Jeremy is home from work. That's almost as surprising as the garage door not opening, since he rarely makes it home before the very moment we're sitting down to dinner, and often much later. He's at least an hour early tonight.

My husband manages a hedge fund in the city, and he works harder than anyone I know, but I respect the fact that even if he has to sometimes miss our family dinner, he is home every single night to put Teddy to bed. Aside from the occasional business trip, of course.

"Daddy will help us figure it out," I tell Teddy.

Teddy nods in agreement. As far as he's concerned, there is *nothing* his father can't do. If someone needed to fly around the earth backward to turn back time, Teddy would volunteer Jeremy for the task.

I climb out of the car, tugging at the yoga pants that always seem to ride up into my butt crack. Then I contort my body into the back seat to release Teddy from his harness, and he rewards me with a gap-toothed grin. He recently lost his first baby tooth, followed by a second soon after, and then two more. He was over-the-moon excited after looking enviously at all the other kids in his class who had already lost teeth, but I mourned the loss of that first one as yet another sign of my precious little boy growing up.

Teddy grabs his SpongeBob backpack, which I'm pretty sure weighs as much as he does, if not slightly more. We head over to the front door of our house, Teddy tilted backward as he attempts to hold up the weight of his backpack. When I put my hand on the doorknob, it doesn't turn, and I swear under my breath.

"You said a bad word, Mommy!" Teddy declares, simultaneously aghast and titillated.

"Sorry," I say quickly. "I didn't mean to."

"What's wrong?" he demands to know.

"The door is locked."

"Why?"

I fumble around in my purse, searching for my keys. Considering I always come in through the garage, where the door is never locked, I rarely use them. But I'm pretty sure they're in here somewhere. "I don't know."

"What are you doing now?"

I look up from my purse and flash Teddy what I hope is a patient smile. Sometimes I think my son expects a running narration of everything that I do, and for the most part, I try to provide it. Teddy's kindergarten teacher told me that he had the best vocabulary in the class, and I think it's because I'm always talking to him. "I'm finding my house keys."

"Are they in your purse?"

"Yes."

"Are you sure?"

"Yes!"

Oh my God, where *are* they? I shove aside a mini water bottle and what feels like the giant rock that Teddy picked up at the park last week and asked me to save because he thought it was "cool." And then, thank God, my fingers close around my key chain. I pull it out triumphantly. "Ta-da!"

Obligingly, Teddy claps.

Whatever is wrong with the garage door, we can save it for later. As always, the parking was out of control at the karate school, which is in a strip mall shared by about a dozen other shops. I drove around the lot for several minutes before locating a spot, just in time for the clouds that had been hovering all afternoon to break open. Over an hour later, my hair is still damp, and my shoes squelch with each step. I want nothing more than a quiet evening with my family.

I fit my key into the lock, but the lock doesn't turn. That's...strange. When I am certain that this key is not functional, I pull it out. I examine the key ring, which contains only two keys. One is the key for the house, and the other is the key for my old medical practice, which I gave up when I decided to be a stay-at-home mom for Teddy. No regrets, but I saved my spare key for nostalgic reasons. In any case, that is definitely not the key to my house. Although I try it, just in case.

Nope. I've got two keys, and neither one of them opens the door to the house.

That's when I notice something else. The lock on the door is shinier than I remember. It looks, in fact, brand new. But to my knowledge, we haven't changed this lock in years. Not since I've been living here.

That's my second clue that something is very wrong.

"What's wrong with the key, Mommy?" Teddy asks.

"I don't know."

"When you put the key in the lock, you are s'posed to turn it," he tells me unhelpfully.

"Yes, I know, Teddy."

"Did you turn it?"

"Yes."

"Maybe turn it again?"

My temple is starting to throb, and I am tired of trying to sort through the mystery of why my key no longer works in the lock. Instead, I ring the doorbell. When nobody comes immediately, I bang on the door with my fist. Then I bang harder.

"Why are you kicking the door, Mommy?" Teddy asks.

"Just making sure Daddy hears us."

Thankfully, a few seconds later, footsteps grow louder behind the door. The lock turns, and my husband is standing before me, wearing his dress shirt unbuttoned up to the collar with no tie. Jeremy turned forty about six months ago, and he looks the best he ever has. He takes care of himself—he's a bit of an exercise guru who wakes up an hour early to go to the gym Tuesdays and Thursdays, and then on the other weekdays, he runs at the park. The sandy brown hair on his head shows no sign of thinning with only a few strands of gray at the temples, his dark-brown eyes are just as intense as they were the day I met him, and his diligent flossing must've paid off, because his teeth are white and perfect. There are creases around his eyes when he smiles, which I find incredibly sexy.

Most of my female friends seem to be barely tolerating their husbands. One of them said they ended up having to make an appointment with a specialist because she'd used headaches as an excuse so many times to get out of sex with her husband. But I don't have that problem. Even after years of marriage, I still get that thrill every time I lay eyes on Jeremy. Our chemistry is as strong as it ever was.

"Daddy!" Teddy hollers as he propels himself at Jeremy, the same way he does every day.

Teddy *worships* his father. Over the Christmas holidays, we took a family trip to Disneyland, and I would say that Teddy's enthusiasm for meeting Mickey Mouse paled compared to his enthusiasm for when his father comes home every night. And Teddy *loves* that mouse.

Jeremy rewards our son with a brilliant smile and heaves him into his arms like he weighs practically nothing, even though I have tweaked my back twice in the last year trying to pick up Teddy. Jeremy is a good father—a *great* father even. It's one of the many things I adore about him.

"Daddy, the door is broken," Teddy says gravely.

"Oh, is it?"

He nods solemnly. It's something Jeremy himself does—the two of them look so much alike when Teddy nods like that. "We couldn't get in!"

I hold up my key as I step into the house. "The key wasn't turning. Did you change the lock?"

My husband hesitates, not answering my question. He lowers Teddy to the floor and cracks open the door to the house. "Teddy," he says. "Could you go up to your room and play quietly? I need to talk to your mom."

If I made such a request, Teddy would quiz me about it for half an hour. But when his father asks him to do it, he immediately trots into the house and goes up to his room without another word. And once he's gone, Jeremy again closes the door to the house and turns to face me.

"Jeremy." I wring my hands together. "What's going on?"

My husband rubs his lower jaw, which is just starting to sprout a shadow from having shaved this morning. He's avoiding my eyes, which is my third clue that something is wrong. My husband does not have any trouble making eye contact. He is the king of eye contact.

"Naomi," he says. "We need to talk."

ACKNOWLEDGMENTS

Since this story was short and sweet (and so am I), I'll keep the acknowledgments short and sweet as well.

Thank you to my advance readers: my mother (as always), Emily, Pam, and Val. Thank you to my agent, Christina, who has helped me negotiate all things Housemaid.

How's that for short and sweet?

ABOUT THE AUTHOR

#1 *New York Times*, Amazon Charts, *Washington Post*, *Wall Street Journal*, *USA Today*, and *Publishers Weekly* bestselling author Freida McFadden is a physician specializing in brain injury. Freida's work has been selected as one of Amazon Editor's Best Books of the Year, and she has been a Goodreads Choice Award nominee. Her novels have been translated into more than forty languages. Freida lives with her family and cat in a centuries-old three-story home overlooking the ocean.